Racing Indy Cars

Racing Indy Cars

George Sullivan

Illustrated with photographs

COBBLEHILL BOOKS   *Dutton*   *New York*

J 796.72 S949r 1992
Sullivan, George, 1927-
Racing Indy cars
                NOV 09 '11

Picture Credits

Indianapolis Motor Speedway (Harry Goode, 54; Ron McQueeney, 50, 53, 56; Steve Swope, 58; Steve Vorhees, 45); © Indy 500 Photos (Ron McQueeney and Ed Kackley), 2; Aime LaMontagne, 41; Michigan International Speedway (K. Coles), 33; Phoenix International Speedway (Tim Rempe), 8, 31. All other photographs are by George Sullivan.

Frontispiece: Indy cars roar down the front straightaway at the start of the famed Indianapolis 500.

Copyright © 1992 by George Sullivan
All rights reserved
No part of this book may be reproduced in any form without permission in writing from the publisher

Library of Congress Cataloging-in-Publication Data
Sullivan, George, date
Racing indy cars/George Sullivan. p. cm. Includes index. ISBN 0-525-65082-2
1. Automobile racing--Juvenile literature. 2. Indianapolis Speedway Race--Juvenile literature. I. Title.
GV1029.S86 1992   796.7′2—dc20   91-19439   CIP   AC

Published in the United States by Cobblehill Books, an affiliate of Dutton Children's Books,
a division of Penguin Books USA Inc. 375 Hudson Street, New York, New York 10014

Designed by Jean Krulis
Printed in Hong Kong
First Edition 10 9 8 7 6 5 4 3 2 1

Acknowledgments

The author is grateful to many individuals who helped him in writing and researching this book. Special thanks are due: Mark Harder, Douglas Shierson Racing; David T. Elshoff, CART; Ron McQueeney, Indianapolis Motor Speedway; Randy Schwoerer, Schwoerer Associates; Frank A. Yodice, FYI Associates; Mark Beal, Marlboro Grand Prix, Meadowlands; John Devaney, and Aime LaMontagne.

Contents

Introduction

Imagine you're squeezed and strapped into the cockpit of a powerful racing car. The fit is so tight, about all you can move are your hands and feet.

When you hit the throttle and the car rockets down the track, it's like you're driving through a tunnel at rush hour. Only everyone is traveling at 200 miles an hour and the drive is going to last 2½ hours.

All you hear is the scream of engines and the screech of tires. Your eyes are on the "groove," the black line of rubber that cars leave on the track. It's the fastest route to travel.

There are few escape roads, few gravel run-off areas. On each side is a wall of concrete about a foot thick. One touch and that wall will tear your wheels off.

You rarely hit the brakes. Even in an emergency, you don't want to come off the throttle fast because you'll upset the delicate balance of the car. You use the corners to wipe off speed, one eye on that wall.

That's what driving an Indy car is like. You have to be brave. You have to be precise. You can never make a mistake. The Indy car is the world's fastest racing machine.

This book takes a closeup look at Indy cars (named after the Indianapolis 500). It explains how they're built and what it costs to build them. It takes a look at a racing team, the engineers and mechanics who prepare a car for a race and keep it running at topmost speeds.

It tells what it's like to drive an Indy car on big, paved ovals and on tortuous road courses. It describes how, in 1990, one driver flew around the famous track at Indianapolis in the fastest time in history.

Overall, the book seeks to capture some of the color and excitement that have made auto racing one of the most popular spectator sports in the world.

The Indy car is the world's fastest racing machine.

1. Indy Cars

An Indy car can go from 0 to 60 in two seconds, from 0 to 100 in 4½ seconds. On a long straightaway, an Indy car can hit 235 mph. That's equal to traveling the length of a football field in just one second.

The Indy car didn't become the world's fastest racer overnight. It has gone through a great deal of change in the past three or four decades.

The Indy car once had its engine in front. Then engineers in Europe developed the rear-engine racer. The first competed at the Indianapolis 500 in 1961.

In a car with its engine in front, the drive shaft, which transmits the engine's power to the wheels, runs under the car to the rear wheels. But with the engine in the rear, no long drive shaft is needed. Rear-engine cars can be built very low to the ground.

No longer did the driver have to sit straight up, blocking the air currents. Now he could be placed low in the car, his feet stretched out into the racer's pointed nose.

Rear-engine cars beat the old front-engine cars in race after race. By 1965, Indy cars with the engines in front had gone the way of spoked wheels and leather helmets.

Early cars that raced at Indianapolis were built of heavy sheet metal. This was replaced by aluminum and carbon fiber. Cars became much lighter and faster as a result.

In fact, cars became so light that at high speeds they tended to lift off the track. Drivers had trouble keeping control.

The solution: wings. Today's Indy car has two wings, one placed behind the engine and the other attached to the car's nose.

These front and back wings, when compared to an

A mechanic in the cockpit, an Indy car is towed from garage area to the track for a practice run.

Car's front and back wings produce downforce, which provides traction and improves handling.

airplane's wings, are mounted upside down. They produce the opposite result of airplane wings. Instead of lifting the car, they press it down against the track. This "downforce," as it's called, provides better traction and makes the car easier to handle.

At one time Indy car racing was as American as apple pie or hot dogs at a baseball game. American drivers raced American cars. Not anymore. As Indy car racing entered the decade of the '90s, some 15 percent of the fifty or so licensed Indy car drivers were foreign-born.

As for the cars, the change has been startling. At the Indianapolis 500 and other Indy car races of the early 1990s, the truly American car was a rarity. The British Lola had taken over as the most popular racer. The Lola features a high windscreen—almost at driver's-eye level—that sweeps down to a wider than average nose. Mario and Michael Andretti, Bobby Rahal, and 1990 Indy 500 winner, Arie Luyendyk, pilot Lolas.

Nine of the ten top cars that qualified to race at

Indy cars don't have speedometers. This dashboard instrumentation reports rpm's as speed boost. (Car's steering wheel was removed for this photo.)

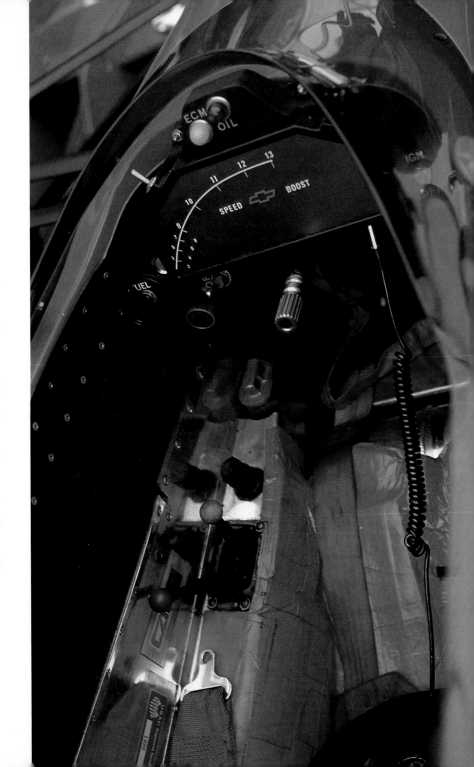

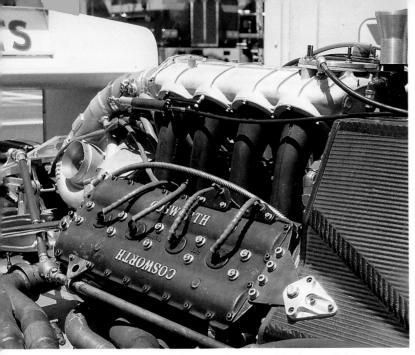

Cosworth-Ford engine once dominated Indy car field.

Indianapolis in 1990 were either Lolas or another popular British car, the Penske. From the side, the Penske looks much like a Lola. But it's built lower than the Lola, has a lower cowl around the driver, a lower windscreen, and a fatter nose. Emerson Fittipaldi and Rick Mears drive Penskes.

Indy car engines are almost as "un-American" as the cars. For years, the standard Indy car engine was the British-built Cosworth-Ford. In recent years, however, the Ilmor-Chevrolet engine, built in England, has proven more popular. It is lighter yet more powerful than the Cosworth.

Ilmor-Chevrolet racing engine proved huge success beginning in the late 1980s.

Rick Mears guides his Penske through a gentle turn at the Meadowlands road course.

All Indy cars have a turbocharged engine. A turbocharger makes a fast car go even faster.

What the turbocharger does is take a blast of the engine's exhaust gases and use it to spin a windmill-like pump. The pump forces great amounts of a fuel-and-air mixture into the engine's combustion chamber. There the mixture is burned.

The greater the volume of fuel-air mixture burned in the combustion chamber, the more power. The more power, the greater the car's speed.

The biggest change in Indy car racing in recent years has been in the use of computers that gather information about the car as it is competing. Sensors in some cars measure twenty to thirty different variables, everything from the car's speed and fuel use to oil pressure and chassis downforce.

Data from the sensors is displayed on a trackside computer screen. During a practice session or race, the screen is constantly being monitored by the team manager, crew chief, engineers, and mechanics. They analyze the data and act upon it.

While today's Indy car driver has a computer telling him exactly how his car and its engine are doing at any point in a race, he still relies on his own senses.

"You're absolutely strapped into the car," says Bobby Rahal, the 1986 winner at Indianapolis. "You're wearing the car. Your back might be telling you something, your fanny, your hands. You're getting all of these feelings through your body."

Derrick Walker, a noted racing team manager, puts it this way: "The seat of the pants is the best computer."

Even though they sometimes travel at undreamed-of speeds, modern-day Indy cars are actually safer than racers of the past. That's because they boast so many safety features.

Engineers once believed that the stronger and heavier the car, the safer it would be. Cars had rigid steel frames and were made of heavy sheet metal. But in such a car, the impact of a crash often caused serious injury to the driver.

In today's Indy cars, the lightweight aluminum and carbon fiber body is actually designed to collapse on impact. The wheels fly off. Instead of somersaulting down the track, the car drops to the ground and slides along its bottom.

The cockpit where the driver is seated is protected by heavy aluminum. It is meant to remain intact. Pad-

Arie Luyendyk gets strapped into cockpit before a practice run.

Padded driver's cockpit is shielded with heavy aluminum. Note rollover hoop mounted behind cockpit.

ding behind the seat absorbs the impact of a rear-end crash.

A sturdy shoulder harness and seat belt hold the driver in place. Besides, there isn't room for any movement in the cockpit. It's such a close fit, in fact, that the driver hasn't room enough to hook up his own seat belt. A mechanic has to help him with it.

An on-board extinguisher spurts out chemicals if a fire breaks out.

The padded steering wheel will collapse on impact.

The driver's helmet is thickly padded. Its plastic visor is shatterproof.

The padded suit the driver wears is made of No-mex, a fire-resistant cloth. He wears a woven hood—called a *balaclava*—beneath his helmet that is also made of Nomex.

The driver's socks and shoes, his gloves, and even his underwear are made of Nomex, too. Should a fire break out, his Nomex clothes give the driver about 30 seconds of protection.

Many structural parts of the car are designed to protect the driver should a crash occur. They include:

Fuel Cell—Located behind the driver and in front of the engine, the fuel cell is a sturdy, rubberlike con-

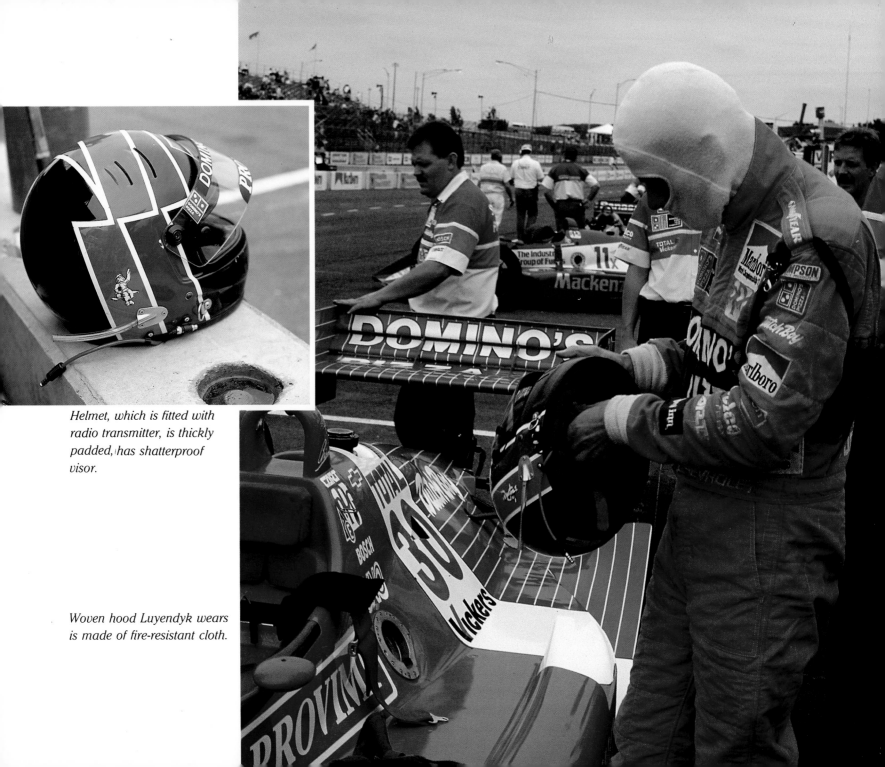

Helmet, which is fitted with radio transmitter, is thickly padded, has shatterproof visor.

Woven hood Luyendyk wears is made of fire-resistant cloth.

tainer filled with spongy material. The spongy material absorbs the fuel and helps to keep it from splashing around in case of a crash. The cell is enclosed in a fuel tank made of heavy-duty aluminum.

Rollover Hoop—This takes the form of a curved metal frame or bar. It's mounted on the car's body just behind the driver's head. Should the car flip over, the hoop acts to protect the driver's head from injury.

Nose—The car's cone-shaped nose absorbs impact by means of a "controlled collapse" in the event of a crash. The driver's feet are further protected by a honeycomb metal panel within the nose.

Sidepods—These are boxlike structures on each side of the car. Each contains a radiator as well as other systems or parts. The sidepods, like the car's nose, are designed to absorb the impact of a crash.

"With the new technology, it's not as dangerous as it used to be," says veteran driver A.J. Foyt. "I'd rather crash these cars at 220 miles an hour than the old cars at 150."

Car's nose is designed to collapse in case of crash, absorbing impact.

2. The Team

The Monday morning headlines after a big race usually go to the driver and the car. But supporting the driver is a skilled team of engineers, mechanics, and other personnel. They're as vital to a driver's success as fuel and the right tires.

Team Shierson, owned by Illinois businessman Robert Tezak, with headquarters in Adrian, Michigan, is one of the most successful teams on the Indy car circuit. The team's car, sponsored by Domino's Pizza and driven by Arie Luyendyk, won the Indianapolis 500 in 1990, setting a new speed record in the process.

The Shierson team of more than a dozen men and one woman is headed by Neil Micklewright, its general manager. A native of Aldridge, England, Micklewright joined Team Shierson in 1983 after eleven years of experience in European racing.

Micklewright is the boss. He manages the team.

During a race, he monitors the team's trackside computer for information on the car's speed, fuel consumption, mileage, rpm's, oil pressure, and water pressure. He's in constant radio contact with Luyendyk. Together they decide when pit stops are to be made.

When Luyendyk does bring the car in, Micklewright is the one person who speaks with him, seeking to solve any problems he might be having. Is there anything the crew can do to make the car perform better? That's what Micklewright wants to find out.

John Dick, the chief engineer, recommends how the car is to be set up, that is, what adjustments should be made to the chassis and wings in preparing the car for the race. Assistant engineer Robert Sack supervises the Shierson team's computer system.

Mike Battersby, the crew chief, is in charge of all the mechanical work. The Shierson team keeps two

Shierson engineers and mechanics ready their car for practice run.

Lolas in operating condition throughout the season. Each is powered by a Chevrolet engine, and has its own lead mechanic. And each lead mechanic has an assistant. These four men do work assigned by Battersby.

A fifth mechanic is responsible for rebuilding and maintaining each car's gearbox.

The team also includes a fabricator. He builds and repairs the wings and any other special parts the car needs.

Mary Mendez, the team's scorer, is the only female member of the team. Posted at a trackside computer console, she keeps track of the car's speed, the number of laps it has run, and its use of fuel.

During a race, she also monitors each of the other cars. She knows the speed of each, its position in the race, and the number of pit stops each has made. This information is used in planning race strategy.

The boardman is yet another member of the team. During a race, he is stationed across the track from the team's pit. His job is to hold up signs bearing messages for Luyendyk. For example, a sign that says "+4" informs Luyendyk he is ahead of the field by four seconds.

Indy cars and their spare parts travel from one race

Mary Mendez, the team's scorer, monitors car's performance at trackside computer console.

course to another in a transporter, a huge tractor-trailer that also serves as a machine shop. The trailer driver and an assistant driver are other members of the crew.

The driver of the transporter not only drives. He also must see to it that the trailer gets stocked with parts, loaded, and, most important, arrives at the track on time.

Domino's Pizza Indy Car

MANUFACTURER:	Lola Cars, Ltd.
MODEL:	T9000
LENGTH:	185 inches
WIDTH:	78.5 inches
WHEELBASE:	110 inches
HEIGHT:	32 inches
WEIGHT:	1,550 pounds
FUEL CAPACITY:	40 gallons
ENGINE:	Ilmor-Chevrolet
HORSEPOWER:	705 at 12,200 rpm
FUEL:	Methanol
STEERING:	Rack and pinion
BRAKES:	Four-caliper, vented-disk
SUSPENSION:	Four-wheel independent push-rod front, push-rod rear
MILEAGE:	1.85 miles per gallon

Mechanic checks tire pressure before qualifying run.

3. What It Costs

The cost of building a car and getting it ready to compete make Indy car racing one of the most expensive of all sports. It takes millions of dollars to purchase a car and engine, keep it fueled, and provide for the salaries and expenses of the driver, members of the race team, and other employees.

The tremendous costs involved are one reason that professional racing teams have sponsors. A sponsor may be an automobile manufacturer, a tobacco company, or a food or beverage company. In return for their financial support, sponsors get to advertise their products on the racing cars and the uniforms of the drivers and team members.

For anyone interested in buying an Indy car and entering it in competition, here's a shopping list:

Race Car—You start with a "rolling chassis," the car's central structure, a tube-shaped shell made of aluminum, carbon fiber, and other durable material and lightweight materials. The chassis includes the steering and suspension systems but not the engine.

You'll need three chassis, not merely one. Two are at the track for each race. The third is being worked on in the shop.

Cost of each: $250,000.

Engine—For each race, you need one engine for practice and qualifying, and another for the race. You also need two or three spares in case any serious problem develops. Most teams, in fact, operate with eight to ten engines per race car.

Cost of each: $60,000 to $80,000.

Wheels—The chassis comes equipped with four wheels, the circular frames upon which the tires fit. For the racing seasons, at least twelve sets will be needed; that's 48 wheels.

Cost per wheel: $2,200.

You need one engine for practice and qualifying, another for the race, plus several spares.

Tires—Tires are expensive because they wear out so fast you need many of them. For a race on a short oval or road course, you'll probably need five or six sets. At the Indianapolis 500 or other 500-mile events, as many as eight or nine sets may be required.

Cost per tire: $150 to $175.

Fuel—Indy cars get no prizes for fuel efficiency. They average 1.8 miles per gallon of fuel.

The fuel is methanol, which provides maximum horsepower without overheating the engine. Methanol is also safer than gasoline. It does not ignite as quickly, reducing the risk of fire in case of a crash.

Cost per car per season: $20,000 to $40,000.

Spare Parts—During the summer and fall racing seasons, each team requires from $300,000 to $400,000 in disposable parts. This includes $50,000 to $75,000 just for gearbox parts.

Transporter—To get your race cars from one event to the next and to all testing sessions, you need a huge

For the Indianapolis 500, or any 500-mile race, eight or nine sets of tires are required.

tractor-trailer, called a transporter. It also serves as a machine shop on wheels, one that's outfitted with a complete inventory of spare parts.

Cost of a fully equipped transporter: $250,000 to $300,000.

Don't forget to include the salaries and living expenses for your driver and the racing team, the engineers, mechanics, and all the others.

Total cost for a year of racing: As much as $5 million.

As many as twelve sets of wheels are needed for the racing season.

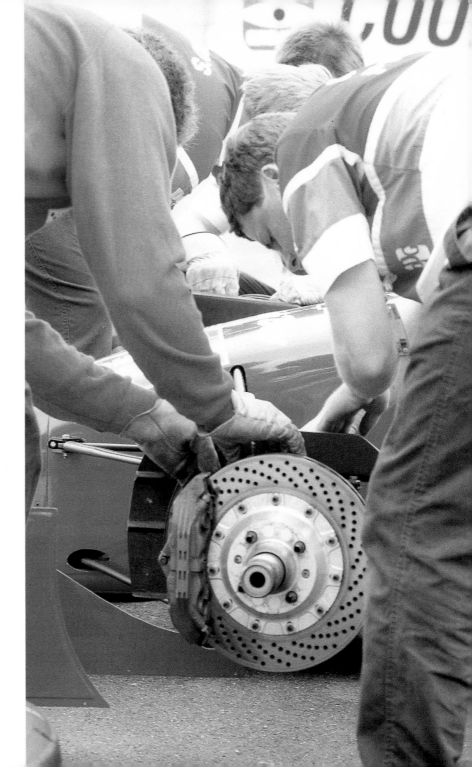

4. The Tracks

Emerson Fittipaldi is one of a small handful of drivers to have won major championships in both Europe and the United States. He says that Indy car racing "is tougher than any other type of racing."

The reason? The tracks.

"You have four completely different types of tracks," Fittipaldi points out, "each of which requires different skills. There's no championship in the world that's like it."

Each year, between March and October, Indy cars compete in sixteen or seventeen races in the United States, Canada, and Australia. The races are sanctioned by CART, short for Championship Auto Racing Teams. CART is to Indy car racing what the National Football League, the NFL, is to pro football. More than $20 million in prize money is at stake.

Of the four different types of tracks on which the cars compete, the big, paved ovals are the best known. There are two of them: the Indianapolis Speedway, a $2\frac{1}{2}$-mile circuit, and the Michigan International Speedway (in Brooklyn, Michigan), which is two miles in length.

Short ovals represent a second type of course. The Pennsylvania International Raceway (in Lower Nazareth Township), one mile in length, is typical of the short oval.

Third, there are permanent road courses, such as the Mid-Ohio Sports Car Course (a few miles west of Lexington, Ohio). It curves and twists for 2.4 miles. It has fifteen turns.

Fourth, there are temporary road courses, which are laid out on public highways, city streets, and parking lots. These, too, have right- and left-hand curves and turns of every imaginable type. The Grand Prix

Cars streak past the start/finish line at the Phoenix International Raceway, a one-mile oval track.

Each race course offers a different challenge. Left to right: the Michigan International Speedway, Pennsylvania International Speedway, Mid-Ohio Sports Car Course, and the street course on which the Grand Prix of Denver is contested.

of Denver is contested on a downtown course that encloses the city's Civic Center Park. It is 1.73 miles long and has sixteen turns.

A tricky road course means a driver has to be very skilled in shifting and braking. On the other hand, a big oval course calls for smooth, steady driving.

The big oval also demands an extra dose of courage. "You're testing the limits of your bravery," Bobby Rahal, one of the top Indy car drivers of all time, once said. Rahal also has competed in road races. Speaking of his first race on an oval, Rahal said: "As a road racer, I thought, 'There's nothing to it. No big deal.' I found out pretty quickly that I was wrong. Going into a corner at 200 mph will get your attention."

In each race, the first driver to finish a certain number of laps is the winner. (A lap is one complete circuit of the track.)

The season's Indy car champion is determined by a point system. Points are awarded following each race, according to the order of finish. This formula is used:

Finish	Points
First	20
Second	16
Third	14
Fourth	12
Fifth	10
Sixth	8
Seventh	6
Eighth	5
Ninth	4
Tenth	3
Eleventh	2
Twelfth	1

Al Unser, Jr., (left) hurries to a victory at the Michigan International Speedway.

One additional point goes to the fastest qualifier in each race and a second additional point is awarded to the driver who led for the most laps.

Cash awards go to the top twenty finishers in the point race. The season's champion receives $500,000.

Recent winners have included Al Unser, Jr., Emerson Fittipaldi, and Danny Sullivan. When Al Unser, Jr., captured the title in 1990, his first, he scored 210 points, becoming the first Indy car driver to break the 200-point record.

5. One Lap on a Road Course

In the days of practice before a race, engineers and mechanics fine-tune their cars to suit the conditions of the track on which they're racing. The right chassis "setup," as it's called, can mean the difference between winning and losing.

The suspension system is critical. Adjustments are made to the springs and other devices that shield the chassis from roadway bumps and shocks. Maybe stiff springs are best. Or maybe the driver wants a "loose" car.

Mechanics tinker with the wings, too. Even the tiniest wing adjustment can be important in how the car performs.

Changing the angle of the front wing by only $1/10$ of a degree might enable the car to get around the track $1/5$ of a second faster. At the end of twenty-five laps, that's a difference of five seconds. And five seconds is a very big chunk of time in a tight race.

Setting up also includes choosing the right tires. Different types of tires are needed for wet and dry conditions. The dry tire has no tread. It's as smooth as the back of your hand. Drivers call dry tires "slicks."

The rain tire has a tread. The tread is designed to get water out from underneath the tire. It gives more grip.

In the case of the Indy 500, where cars make only left-hand turns, tires of different sizes are used. The tires on the left wheels are slightly smaller in circumference than the right tires. This causes the car to roll naturally to the left.

Throughout the race, the driver and crew members have to watch the tires and track conditions constantly. Suppose a car is running on rain tires and the track starts to dry out. The rain tires begin heating up.

They can get so hot that chunks of rubber start to fly off. Naturally, the crew has to change to slicks before that starts to happen.

Even a slight shift in weather conditions can change a car's performance. During the time trials at Indianapolis before the 1990 race, Bobby Rahal ran a lap at 225 miles an hour, a sizzling pace. On another run two days later, Rahal's speed dropped off to 220. The car was set up the same way each time. Rahal blamed added humidity on the day of the second run for slowing him down.

During the race, as the fuel tank empties or the track gets slicker, a driver can use levers to adjust the car's sway bars. These help to stabilize the car. To a great extent, racing is a matter of adjusting. It never stops.

The driver is much more of a factor on a road course than on an oval. With all the shifting, braking, and turning the driver must do, he plays a bigger role. Every road course is a tough challenge from beginning to end.

Take the Meadowlands Grand Prix, for example, a

Choosing the right tires for a race is always a critical matter.

182.2 mile, 150-lap Indy car contest. It's raced on a 1.2-mile, six-turn course laid out on the roads and parking lots of the New Jersey Sports Complex in East Rutherford. The New York City skyline serves as a backdrop for the race.

When the green flag falls and you come across the start/finish line, hit the throttle hard. Ease to the right as you pass under the pedestrian bridge, still hard on the throttle.

The trickiest spot on the track is coming up, a sweeping left-hand turn. Back off the throttle as you approach the turn, keeping far to the right. Without touching the brakes, downshift to fourth.

There's a gentle hill at this point. It's banked to the inside, which helps you to hold the corner. You're at 130 mph or so.

Don't ease off the throttle. Simply let the car slip toward the right-hand wall, which puts you into perfect position as you hit the high-speed back straightaway.

This is the fastest part of the course. Hit the throttle and shift into fifth. You should get up to 190 or 200

A driver's view of the Meadowlands track. Numbered signs at right aid drivers in deciding when to shift.

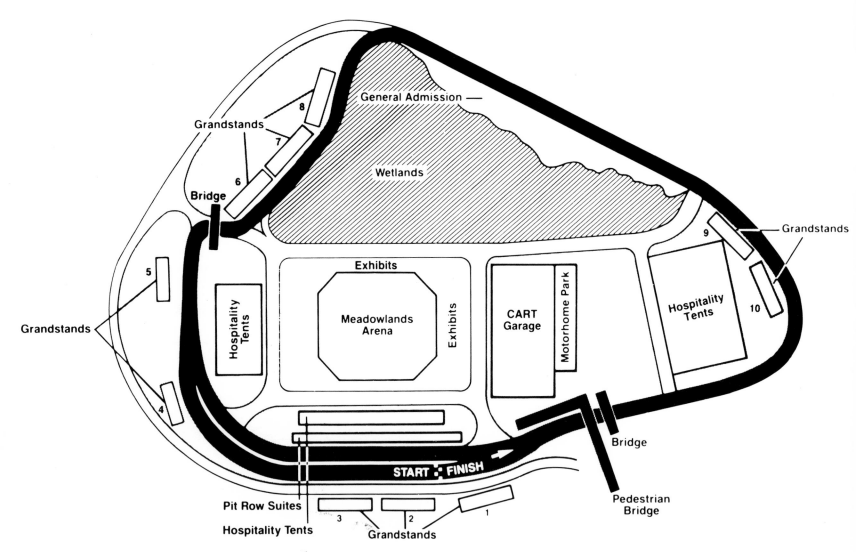

The Meadowlands course is 1.2 miles in length, has six turns.

mph. Get ready to hit the brakes hard for the wetlands turn.

Stay to the right as you come off the straight. As you hit the brakes, downshift from fifth to second. Your speed drops to around 65 mph.

As you come out of the turn, aim for the kink by grandstand 8. Do it right and the kink will seem almost straight. Shift from second to fourth as fast as you can move the shift lever.

As you pass grandstand 6, move over to the left edge of the track. You should be moving at about 120 mph. Again, squeeze the brakes and downshift from fourth to first. Twist the wheel far to the left for the pit-row turn.

Accelerate and shift up through fourth. You should be hugging the wall as you reach grandstand 4. Your speed is around 135 mph.

Keep to the right as you pass grandstand 3, shifting into fifth as soon as you are able. Watch for traffic coming out of the pit exit. Also be on the lookout for cars trying to pass you on your right.

Sway bars (topmost strut) can be adjusted from the cockpit by the driver.

Proper adjustment of suspension system is key factor in how car performs.

Mechanics change setting of rear wing before practice session.

Michael Andretti, winner of the race in 1990, hurries through a Meadowlands' turn.

Start moving to the right as you pass start/finish and get set to go around again.

If you did everything right, you should have zipped around the track in less than 35 seconds. Now you have to do it another 149 times.

You can't have any problems with your pit stops. And, of course, there can't be any incidents with other cars.

All this, plus a little luck, and the trophy and the winner's purse are yours.

6. Pit Stop . . . 16 Seconds

Arie Luyendyk pulls his bright red, white, and blue racer into his pit and hits the brakes. Even before the car has come to a full stop, the six members of his pit crew have scrambled over the low concrete wall separating the track from the spectators. They swarm about the car, each with a specific job to do. Here is a second-by-second account of a successful pit stop:

:01

The air-jack man inserts an air hose in an opening on the top of the car. Compressed air presses down on four metal plates near each wheel. The plates raise the car from the ground. Crew chief Michael Battersby starts inspecting the car for damage.

:02

The vent man attaches a vent hose to the top of the fuel cell behind the cockpit. The vent hose permits air from the fuel cell to escape so the fuel will go in faster. The refueler inserts the fuel hose into a circular opening on the left side of the car. Fuel starts flowing.

:03

As Neil Micklewright, the team's general manager, crouches down to confer with Luyendyk, a crew member hands Luyendyk a squeeze bottle filled with water.

:04

Tire changing is underway. A mechanic is assigned to each wheel. Wielding high-speed power wrenches, they remove the single lug nut holding each wheel in place.

:05

Each 40-pound wheel is removed. Crew members have to be careful in handling wheels. Bouncing or rolling a tire can be considered a violation of safety rules. A team can be penalized as a result.

:06

Bare hubs are covered with new wheels, and tires.

:07

With a flick of a switch, power wrenches are reversed and the wheels with the new tires are tightened on their hubs.

:08

Crew members clear any debris that may have accumulated from the air intakes of the car's sidepods.

:09

As refueling is completed, crew members disconnect the fuel coupler, automatically resealing the fuel cell.

:10

Fuel hoses are handed to crew members behind the pit wall.

:11

With new wheels in place, tire changers grab for any tools or loose equipment used during the stop.

At Indy 500, Shierson crew hurries to refuel the car, change tires.

:12

Crew members carry hoses and other equipment over the pit wall. Tires can scatter any objects left behind, creating a hazard. A team can be penalized for anything left in the pit.

:13

To avoid a stall, the car must be pushed out of the pit for a short distance as it is being restarted. Crew members start moving toward the rear of the car to begin pushing.

:14

Luyendyk tosses his plastic water bottle over the pit wall and gets ready to pull out of the pit. His eyes are focused on a stop sign held in front of the car by one of the crew.

There's no cap on the spout of an Indy car fuel tank. Fuel nozzle goes into self-sealing circular opening in car's side.

Opposite: To avoid a stall, cars are pushed after a pit stop to get them going.

:15

Other crew members have taken their positions behind the car. The stop sign goes down. Everyone pushes.

:16

The car gains momentum, then screeches down the pit road and out onto the track.

7. The Fastest Indy Ever

The Indianapolis 500 is the most famous of all Indy car races. It is to auto racing what the World Series is to baseball or the Super Bowl is to pro football.

The race is held on Memorial Day weekend at the Indianapolis Motor Speedway, a 2½-mile oval. The first driver to complete 200 laps—a distance of 500 miles—wins the race. More than $1 million in prize money goes to the winner.

The Indianapolis Speedway was built in 1909. The first Indy 500 was held two years later.

In its original design, the track had a domino shape—two long straightaways and two short ones. The four turns were very sharp and not banked much. The slight banking meant that a speeding car, when rounding a turn, tended to drift high on the track.

In the years since it opened, the track at Indianapolis has undergone many changes. The paving bricks that formed the original surface have been covered over with blacktop. A concrete wall, almost 3 feet in height, now surrounds the track. Guardrails and safety fences have been built to protect spectators.

Despite all the changes, the character of the track has not changed much. It still features those long straightaways and sharp turns.

The number of cars that compete in the race is limited to thirty-three. At the start, they line up in eleven rows, three cars to a row.

To earn a position in the race—to "qualify"—drivers compete in time trials.

Each driver gets three chances to qualify. On each attempt, he does four laps (ten miles) at top speed.

His car is clocked by an automated timing system. The thirty-three cars with the fastest average speed for the four laps qualify.

The fastest car of all in the qualifying laps wins the inside starting position in the first row. This is known

as the pole position. Because the inside route offers the shortest distance around the track, the pole position has a built-in advantage.

In fact, through 1990, thirteen drivers had won the Indy 500 from the pole position. There had been no winners from farther back than 28th.

Qualifying laps are much faster than race laps. After all, the driver is alone on the track. There are no other cars to worry about. The driver can focus on speed, and speed only.

In 1988, Rick Mears, when qualifying, became the first driver to officially reach 220 miles per hour at Indianapolis. Mears had a one-lap run of 220.453 mph. For the four laps, he averaged 219.198 mph.

When the cars lined up for the 74th running of the Indianapolis 500 in 1990, thirty-six-year-old Arie Luyendyk, starting in the first row with the third fastest qualifying time—223.304 mph—was not among the favorites. There were eight former Indy 500 winners in the race that year, and five or six of them were considered more likely to win than Luyendyk.

In past races at Indianapolis, Luyendyk had been no shining star. He had started five times. Finishing seventh was the best he had ever done there.

Luyendyk's overall Indy car record was not very bright, either. Arriving in the United States from his native Holland in 1981, Luyendyk had been racing on the Indy car circuit since 1984. He had competed in 75 races. He had never won.

Nevertheless, as he awaited the starter's flag, Luyendyk was confident. His confidence had begun to build late in 1989 when he had joined Shierson racing, a team formerly owned by Texas oilman Douglas Shierson, its cars sponsored by Domino's Pizza. Team Shierson had a reputation as one of the best in Indy car racing.

Luyendyk was impressed with the team right from the beginning. In every race leading up to Indianapolis, the team had given him a car that was not merely very fast but also safe.

Another reason for Luyendyk's confidence was the car he was driving, a Lola. It was powered by a turbocharged Chevrolet racing engine. Since 1988, cars with Chevy engines had been winning about everything in sight. The engine seemed unbeatable. At last, Luyendyk felt, he had the right equipment.

When the green flag fell, Emerson Fittipaldi, who had started in the pole position, charged into the lead. He was still leading after ten laps. Bobby Rahal, driv-

Led by a trio of yellow pace cars, the thirty-three racers get underway at the Indianapolis 500.

ing another Lola-Chevy, was second, about a quarter of a mile back. Luyendyk was third.

Al Unser, Jr., Mario Andretti, and Rick Mears were fourth, fifth, and sixth.

Like the other drivers, Luyendyk was trying to run a steady race—hitting speeds of 230 to 235 on the long straightaways, backing off a bit on the turns. He knew not to push the car too much in the early laps because he wanted to be there at the end. It is in the last 40 or 50 laps that the Indy 500 is lost or won. That's when you have to run your strongest.

Luyendyk had handling problems with his car in the early stages. The front tires were hard to control; the car had too much "push," a tendency to keep going straight when Luyendyk wanted to turn left. Even after a wing adjustment, he still had push. A tire change finally solved the problem.

Luyendyk then turned up the speed, taking over the lead from Fittipaldi and holding it for a couple of laps. Rahal was first for five laps. But it was Fittipaldi who dominated the first 135 laps of the 200-lap race, leading in 128 of them.

Then fate took a hand. The track, which had been cool and easy on tires, started to heat up under sunny skies. Tires started to heat up, too.

Fittipaldi was the first to be affected. His overheated right rear tire began to blister. The blistering made the tire vibrate dangerously. Fittipaldi had to make an extra pit stop for new tires.

Bobby Rahal took over the lead. Now Luyendyk was second. Fittipaldi dropped back to third.

Little by little, Luyendyk, who had trailed Rahal by as much as a quarter of a mile, closed the gap. The two snaked their way past several slower cars, Rahal in front, Luyendyk just behind, the red nose of his Lola practically touching Rahal's racer.

As the two cars tore down the back straightaway, Luyendyk decided to make his move. He flashed ahead of Rahal and into the lead as they rounded the turn. "As he went by," Rahal would say later, "he was going like a bat out of hell."

Rahal made his final pit stop on lap 171. Luyendyk went in on lap 173.

When Luyendyk pulled back out, he was just ahead of Rahal. Then Luyendyk took charge, turning up the speed. He blazed down the straightaways and rocketed around the corners. When he checked his mirrors, Rahal was no longer there.

Luyendyk felt certain that victory was within his grasp. "I knew," he would say later, "that if nothing

Bobby Rahal makes a pit stop on his way to victory in the 1986 Indy 500.

On Indianapolis straightaways, Luyendyk hit speeds of 230 plus.

funny happened, I should be able to do it."

Nothing funny happened. Luyendyk streaked away to cross the finish line 10.7 seconds ahead of Rahal. "When I took the checkered flag, I went nuts inside my helmet," he said.

Not only did Luyendyk win, but he did so with the fastest average speed in the history of the Indy 500— 185.984 mph. The previous record, set by Rahal in 1986, was 170.722 mph.

With his victory, Luyendyk won instant worldwide recognition and respect. Robin Miller, writing in the *Indianapolis Star*, put it like this: "It was a great triumph for a deserving driver whose equipment finally caught up with his talent."

On his way to victory, Luyendyk averaged 185.984 miles per hour, cutting almost 15 minutes off the record.

Luyendyk car is on souvenir jackets awarded team members.

Luyendyk and scores of well-wishers celebrate his Indy win.

Racing Words and Terms

Balaclava—The snug-fitting, fire-resistant hood worn by drivers under their helmets.

Banking—The slope of a track, particularly on the turns.

CART—An acronym for Championship Auto Racing Teams, the governing body of Indy car racing.

Chassis—The frame and wheels of a car upon which the body rests. Also called the tub.

Drive shaft—In a car with the engine in front, the rotating shaft that transmits the engine's power to the rear wheels.

Groove—The easiest and fastest route around a race course.

Horsepower—The unit for measuring the power of an engine.

Lap—One complete circuit of a race track. Also, to get ahead of an opponent in a race by one or more complete circuits of the track.

Methanol—Methyl alcohol; the fuel used to power an Indy car.

Pace car—The automobile that leads the race cars through the initial lap of a race but does not compete in the race.

Pit—The area at a race track set aside for refueling and minor repairs.

Pitman—A member of the pit crew.

Pole position—The position on the inside of the front row at the beginning of a race.

Rollover hoop—The sturdy, oval-shaped metal frame behind the driver that acts to prevent injury in the case of a rollover.

Set up—The preparation by the crew of a car for a race.

Sidepods—Compartments on the sides of the car that house the radiator and oil-cooling system. The sidepods also serve to protect the driver in the case of a sideways collision.

Superspeedway—An oval race track at least two miles in length. The Indianapolis Speedway and Michigan International Speedway are superspeedways.

Sway bars—Metal struts from the wheels to the chassis that control sideways movement of the car.

Transporter—A tractor-trailer used for hauling race cars. It also serves as a machine shop and storage area for spare parts.

Tub—*See* Chassis.

Turbocharger—A device that uses the car's exhaust gases to force extra amounts of an air/fuel mixture into the engine for added power and speed.

Wings—Narrow rectangular surfaces mounted at the front and rear of Indy cars that are meant to improve handling and increase stability.

Index